Evincepub Publishing

Parijat Extension, Bilaspur, Chhattisgarh 495001
First Published by Evincepub Publishing 2020
Copyright © Ananya Gulati 2020
All Rights Reserved.

ISBN: 978-93-90362-90-5
Price: /-

This book has been published with all reasonable efforts taken to make the material error-free after the consent of the author. No part of this book shall be used, reproduced in any manner whatsoever without written permission from the author, except in the case of brief quotations embodied in critical articles and reviews. The Author of this book is solely responsible and liable for its content including but not limited to the views, representations, descriptions, statements, information, opinions and references ["Content"]. The Content of this book shall not constitute or be construed or deemed to reflect the opinion or expression of the Publisher or Editor. Neither the Publisher nor Editor endorse or approve the Content of this book or guarantee the reliability, accuracy or completeness of the Content published herein and do not make any representations or warranties of any kind, express or implied, including but not limited to the implied warranties of merchantability, fitness for a particular purpose. The Publisher and Editor shall not be liable whatsoever for any errors, omissions, whether such errors or omissions result from negligence, accident, or any other cause or claims for loss or damages of any kind, including without limitation, indirect or consequential loss or damage arising out of use, inability to use, or about the reliability, accuracy or sufficiency of the information contained in this book.

The Friendship Squad and the Mystery of the Missing Pupils

ANANYA GULATI

ILLUSTRATED BY – ADWITA ANUP KHOBRAGADE

About The Book

My book "The Friendship Squad and the Mystery of the Missing Pupils" will take you on a wonderful ride with diverse characters. In the book, I have attempted to showcase the values of the Bhagavad Gita via funny fiction. A boy named Karan is in a dilemma when his sister is abducted. His best friend Krish supports and encourages him to use his ability to save his beloved sister. Read the book to find out more…

About The Author

Ananya Gulati is eleven years old and has an interest in reading and writing, which is a result of the motivation she received from her teachers in England. She has written many poems, essays, and tales at school for which she has been awarded the "Star of the week". After reading Bhagavad Gita and receiving direction from her parents, she thought of writing fiction with teachings from the holy book. It is a must-read for all the kids at all the levels.

Ananya wrote this book in two months, during the lockdown period, to gift to her father on his birthday, which he thought was a heart-touching moment. Apart from reading and writing Ananya loves to play badminton and is a green belt in martial arts.

Acknowledgement

This book is a work of fiction. The name of people, places, events, organisations, cities, characters, and incidences are fictional and just the product of imagination. Any resemblance to some real event, place or person is entirely coincidental.

No creative work can be done single-handedly. I want to thank all those who helped me in some way
or the other to complete this task.

Firstly, I am thankful to the Almighty for showering his blessings on me and guiding me towards the right path. Next, I would give my thanks to my parents Mrs. Teena Gulati, my mother, and Mr. Sanjeev Gulati, my father, for motivating and guiding me throughout the process of writing the book. Also, I would like to thank Mrs. Anupama Dalmia for helping me find the right publisher. My gratitude to Evincepub Publishing, who helped me in fulfilling my dream and taking this story to numerous readers across the country. My thanks to my editor, Mrs Dola Basu Singh for providing helpful feedback to me and for looking at every minor or major mistake I had made. A heartful thanks to my teachers Miss Sihota and Miss Menton from Hounslow Town Primary School, London for nurturing my hidden talent of writing and taking me to a level I never expected to be in.

Contents

1. The Shimmering Jill Society 1
2. The Unique Family 5
3. Superb School 10
4. Absent Pupils 14
5. The Unrevealed Truth 19
6. The Discussion Begins 22
7. The Conversation Continues 27
8. The Conversation Is Still Not Over! 30
9. The Plan Works 33
10. Happiness Returns 36

THE SHIMMERING JILL SOCIETY

Welcome to The Shimmering Jill Society. It is a lovely place to be in, and the people are charming and delightful. Whenever there is a problem, they solve it together as they appreciate the fact that collaboration is a great skill to have. Want to know how the society got its name? Well, since all the residents are all content with their lives, God smilingly blesses them every year by doing a Money Rain mid-March. The society considers this event as a grand festival. Sweet and savory treats are made, dances and plays are performed, and everybody gathers to celebrate this wonderful event. The people also play a game while the rain falls. And the game goes like this:

Everybody collects as much money as they can in only thirty seconds. After the timer is up, each person's money gets weighed and the person with the most money wins. Every year they have different prizes for the winners. But do not think that the money collected by each person is given to them only. No! All the money goes to the main reception and anybody from the society can take the money anytime they need it. They also use the money to help other societies if they are in need.

Shimmering Jill Society was also admired by other societies, and every year a special guest—like a famous actor or a singer—came to visit them.

If you would have lived there, you would have felt like it is a small friendly village. It had a beautiful playground for the kids and a club for the residents. Both the places were quite popular amongst all the children.

So many years had passed, but the club manager had never changed. He was a soft-spoken, tall man with a French moustache named Mr. Gulati. His amiable nature made every child and adult smile. I surely cannot forget to tell you the incident of the stuck lift! So, what happened was that two cute but naughty children came out of their judo class that took place in the club. Consequently, they decided to go in the lift. One of the children advised that they should stop the lift in the middle, but he was just kidding. Not understanding the joke, the other child pressed the button for the lift to stop in the middle of nowhere! The silly children did not even know how to start the lift again and one of them started crying.

"Now what to do?" said the child who had pressed the button.

"I don't know!" wailed the other one.

"What do you mean? You told me to press the button."

"I was just kidding. Duh." The kids continued to argue.

Meanwhile, a friendly little girl who was playing nearby and had seen the children with a little light, sprinted to the reception and told the manager everything. Luckily, the manager came and told the kids which button to press to run the elevator again. And guess which button it was? Ha! It was the same button that was used to stop the lift. Wasn't that funny?

You should never do this kind of thing as those children got a stern told-off by their parents. There was also a funny but fat ice-cream seller called Raj in the society. He used to entertain the children and make delicious flavors of ice-cream. Some of the flavors he invented on his own like the mouth-watering *Watercoclak* ice-cream and the *Misusrein* ice-cream.

You, my friend, would be truly fortunate to have these scrumptious flavors of ice-cream!

THE UNIQUE FAMILY

In this amazing society resided a family of four. Although all the society was wonderful, this family was immensely popular amongst all the residents. You see dear reader, their love, their generosity, and their kind nature were loved by everyone.

In this family lived an eight-year-old boy named Karan. Karan's friends and teachers could tell that he has done something right with their eyes closed. With his slim body, he kept running all day to help everyone. He was always ready to sprint and help the teachers. And every time he did something he was not supposed to do, a naughty grin would spread on his face, ear to ear. Karan also had sister elder to him called Tanya.

She was remarkably like Karan. Tanya had won many programming competitions and was a champion in her class. The girl also had dozens of friends who she loved to play with.

Her sports skills were to be known by everyone and whenever she had a badminton racket in her hand all the people would know that the opponent is going to be smacked with a big old zero!

Their dad Mr. Khanna was a scientist working on an invention that was ready to launch in one month. And their mum's (Mrs. Khanna) exquisiteness made her the top model of the country.

Now, dear reader, time to get excited because this is when our story starts. It was a Sunday morning, the most relaxed day of all when everyone is unwinding themselves. It was 10:00 in the morning and Tanya and Karan had just woken up.

They checked the calendar, and saw that the date was 15th March, which we all know was the day of the Money Rain. Tanya and all her friends had planned to do the arrangements for the club.

They had even started decorating the lobby for their tower, which looked gorgeous with all the balloons and ribbons.

On the other hand, Karan was preparing for a dance performance that used all the dance moves he had learned in school. Getting excited, Karan rapidly wore his costume, which looked great on him.

"Are you ready to witness the greatest performance in the world?" spoke Karan to the audience, standing up with pride.

"Yea, yes!" Loud cheers came from the audience. Everybody seemed to be extremely excited about the day, and why should they not? After all, their happiness has given them this cool festival.

"And now calling our beloved Karan to perform an amazing dance on the song Shot Gun." The festivities continued with Karan's dance performance.

A few hours had passed, and the club manager had also started speaking about the third performance, which Karan's group were going to perform. The performance was quite good really—except the bit when Karan's friend Ben accidentally smacked him on his face.

The day was a lot of fun and now everybody was very tired. They wanted to go to sleep as they had an even busy working day tomorrow.

SUPERB SCHOOL

The moon changed into the sun, and Tanya and Karan were all ready to go to school the next day. Waiting for the school bus, Karan, Ben, and Richard were playing the 'guess my mind' game but suddenly they heard a honk.

Peep! Peep! Peep!

It was the bus. As everyone dashed to get in so they do not need to stand, Karan slipped. When everyone came back to make sure he was alright, he got up and dashed in to get the first seat. You see how naughty he was!

Finally, after all the mess and with a little bit of scolding that Tanya gave to Karan, they reached school.

Their school was an enormous yellowish building that said in bold letters:

LETARTH PUBLIC SCHOOL

As Karan silently walked into the corridor, he leapt up with shock.

"Oh no, now what to do!" he shouted. It was the day of the English exam and Karan had not even touched his book.

On the other hand, Tanya had a mathematics exam she had worked her fingers to the bone for this one and had also reminded Karan, but he had only said:

"Oh, leave it for now, sis. I have got to prepare for my dance performance."

Karan was now feeling silly about what he had done. He stepped into the class with a shiver.

"Karan you are so late today. What happened my dear? Come, have a seat and take out a sharpened pencil," spoke his English teacher Miss Rania, taking a sip from her cup of black tea.

"Okay, Miss Rania," Karan kept his bag on the hanger and sat down. Miss Rania told Olivia to hand out the papers and Richard to hand out the pencils.

"Now your time starts. 3…2…1…GO."

All the children opened their papers and began writing. Karan tapped on his best friend Sahil's back and whispered, "Can you tell me the answer of the first question?"

"Okay. The answer is 'were.' You should know the past tense of 'was,' shouldn't you?"

While this was happening, Tanya was having quite a good exam as she had attempted all the questions and was pleased with herself.

Both the exams finished, and the bell rang for break time.

Ding! Dong!

Tanya and Karan met each other, and Tanya asked her little brother, "How did your exam go, champ?"

"It went just fine, sis," he replied taking a deep breath.

By the way, I forgot to tell you that Karan's favorite teacher was Miss Rania and for Tanya, it was always Mrs. Sarah.

Mrs. Sarah was a pleasant and caring teacher—or at least that's what she showed to everybody. She would spend time with children in her class and whenever a child felt lonely, she had made them feel comfortable. Also, she did not leave them alone and would find a friend for them whenever they needed.

And Miss Rania? You have met her during the test. She was fantastic. She was a profoundly good teacher with always a broad smile on her face.

ABSENT PUPILS

"Missing? Who is missing from my school?" shouted Mr. Raffle, the headteacher of the school, stamping his hands on the table.

It was the next day and back in the head teacher's office, Mr. Raffle had received a piece of regretful news about children getting missing from outside the gate of the school. Mr. Tumpkin was staring blankly at Mr. Raffle's face. He did not know what to say.

"Ah…Ah, Mr. Raffle…I think…" spoke Mr. Tumpkin, shivering.

"Stop waffling and speak clearly."

Gaining the courage to speak, Mr. Tumpkin rapidly shot all the words out of his mouth. "Five children went missing from the school gate. They did not reach home and did not come to school the next day also."

"What are you talking about? How am I going to show my face to all the parents? I command you to make the school rules even more strict. That's the only way to find out who is the kidnapper. Wait a minute, let me write the rules."

He quickly grabbed his pen and a blank piece of paper and started scribbling the rules on it. It took him no longer than one minute and the new rules said:

The New School Rules

1. Pupils cannot go to the toilet alone. They should be accompanied by a teacher or two other children.
2. Break times stand cancelled. Students to eat their lunch in class.
3. The children would be allowed to have fun in class, but no stepping outside for fun.

4. No teacher can send children out to get the attendance register or for any other jobs.
5. No child can go alone at the end of the day.

If any of these rules are not followed, the children or even teachers will be given a detention for four or more hours.

Mr. Raffle explained to Mr. Tumpkin that he must make multiple copies of the rules and hand it out to each class. Then he should tell the class teachers to hand out the rules to every single child.

Mr. Tumpkin obeyed the headmaster and handed out the papers. He also put one copy of the new school rules on the school notice board. But on that paper, the new rules went like this:

The New School Rules

1. Pupils can go to the toilet alone. They should not be accompanied by a teacher or other children.
2. Break times stand cancelled. Students to eat their lunch in class.
3. The children would be allowed to have fun in class, but no stepping outside for fun.

4. No teacher can send children out to get the attendance register or for any other jobs.
5. The only children who go home alone are allowed. Rest everybody must stay near the teacher.

If any of these rules are not followed, the children or even teachers will be given a detention for four or more hours.

Later that day, Karan needed to go to the toilet, so his teacher Miss Rania told him to hurry up. The principal was on a round around the school to check everything was alright. Suddenly, he saw Karan out in the toilet alone and shouted "DETENTION."

Karan was quiet for a moment. It took him some time to understand the words. Then he dared to open his mouth and said, "Why sir?"

"Because you have not been following the rules."

Karan did not have a mind to argue as he knew Mr. Raffle was worried about the school. So, he said sorry and accepted his punishment.

While this was happening, Tanya did not seem to be anywhere. It was like she had disappeared into thin air. Tanya was last seen when the rules were getting handed out. As soon as Karan got this news, he knew it must have been the kidnappers who did this, and big tears began to flow down his eyes. He had to know who the kidnappers were.

While Karan was having this hard day at school, a new family was coming into the society. Karan's family already knew them, and their son Krish was Karan's best friend. The new family also had a daughter named Anaya who was an exceptionally good friend of Tanya.

THE UNREVEALED TRUTH

The school ended, and Karan made way to the detention room. But suddenly he leapt up with shock as he saw something sparkling on the ground. At first, he did not notice what it was but after he did it was impossible to mistaken it. The sparkly thing was his sister's favorite bracelet that he had gifted her on her last birthday.

He picked it up and ran toward his class. There he saw Miss Rania marking the papers. Karan knew that Miss Rania couldn't be the kidnapper as she was the only one in the school. Upon reaching his class, he heard whispers coming from the toilet. He tiptoed to the basin and saw Mr. Tumpkin and Mrs. Sarah. They had a huge sack that1 could easily fit a child in.

"Today we got Tanya, Mr. Tumpkin. We must earn more money, so collect as many children as you can. Let's sell them abroad to an orphanage so we can earn more money from the people who adopt them."

Karan could not believe his eyes or his ears.

"Ok Mrs. Sarah, let's get on with it." They wore their masks and were getting ready to come out of the stinky toilet. Karan moved a step and then ran outside.

Bash!

He bumped into the bin, but the boy did not stop running. Unfortunately, in a hurry, he had left his school hat behind that said KARAN in big, bold letters on it.

"It's that boy Karan, Mrs. Sarah. He was listening to us. We have got to get him first. Leave everything else and concentrate on him."

The now-sweaty Karan reached the detention office.

"Huh! Huh!"

"Why are you huffing and puffing Karan, and why so late kid?" questioned—or sort of demanded—the headmaster.

Karan's lips were stuck. He was out of words again. He tried to tell the truth but stopped. There was no way Karan was going to complain about his schoolteachers without solid proof.

He was confused and upset. At home, he sat on his bed looking miserable. He did not know what to do. That night, his father called the school but without luck.

Now Karan had only one choice: he should consult his only guide and friend Krish.

THE DISCUSSION BEGINS

Well, I have not told you much about Krish before. So here you go. Krish was a nice, decent boy who was one year older than Karan. They were cousins and Krish was nothing short of a miracle. He was an avatar of Lord Vishnu Himself. Krish had many friends but he was extremely naughty as well. Can you guys guess what his favorite food was? Oh, come on! Think... Think… It was butter!

I cannot waste my time telling about Krish now… Mate, Karan is in a big dilemma!

"Krish, Krish!" Karan ran to him, calling his name every now and then.

"Oh, Krish, where are you my friend?" Karan ran to the playground and saw a beautiful sight—all the birds and animals were gathered around Krish, listening to Krish playing a beautiful tune on his flute. He stopped!

"What happened Karan? Were you looking for me?"

"Yes, yes I was. I need you, my friend. Don't you know what happened?"

"First, calm down and have a seat," Krish said, shuffling down to the side of the bench he was sitting on.

"Ok…So what has happened, dear Karan?" Krish spoke again.

"My sister has been kidnapped by her favorite teachers, and only I know about it. But Mrs. Sarah also knows that I have heard it all. I do not know what to do. They are my teachers so how can I complain about them to the headmaster? And there is no point being the best at investigating in the whole class." Karan shot these words out of his mouth without taking a pause.

Krish's eyebrows disappeared into his blue hat. He looked rather disappointed with his friend.

"What?" Horripilation took over Karan. He suddenly looked unsure of Krish's reaction. "Am I not the best?"

"Calm down, bro." giggled Krish. "I was just pulling your leg. Can't believe you fall for it every time." Karan gave back one of his rusty smiles and then it got silent. Pin-drop silence. Both friends sat staring at each other blankly.

Karan broke it. "No time for jokes. Please tell me the right way."

"Well, it is simple. Just look for the clues and tell the headmaster."

"It is not that simple. It is impossible for me. How can I hand over one of my teachers to the headmaster? I will be no good, Krish. Do you know what will happen to them? They will be locked up in prison for life and get beaten by those big thorny sticks."

Krish stopped for a minute and then scolded his friend, "Shame on you, Karan!"

The words were whispered, but there was no regret in Krish's tone.

"Greatest investigator in the class, you call yourself! The best brother and student! Ha!"

Karan lowered his head.

"Oh, you know, Karan that you are fighting for the right. This is the time to show your brightness to the world. You do not have time to think about it now. What will happen to your sister if you don't take action?"

Krish paused and waited for a reaction from his friend. But no luck; Karan sat staring at him dumbly.

"This is a complete disaster for a child like you. Don't you want your sis back, playing with you? Enough of you groaning like this."

"Please stop, Krish," begged Karan. "Do you know what sin you are asking me to do by destroying my teachers? How is this a noble thing to do?" Karan stopped. His arguments were weak in front of Krish's, even to his own ears.

Karan came from a bloodline of people who always knew the right thing to do and never left the battlefield.

But the alternative—fighting with the teachers most dear to him—was equally terrible than not saving his sister.

"Krish, I do not know what to do. Please guide me" Karan guarded his chin up. "But before you speak to let me tell you one thing. I trust your judgement, but I should be fully convinced by your point of view."

Krish smiled. "Listen then, my dearest Karan…"

The Conversation Continues

"The trick," said Krish, "is to do our duty with single-minded focus and great sincerity, without worrying about the results."

Karan gulped. What Krish was saying seemed simple in theory, but how easy was it in practice?

"The trick is not to think about whether you will fail or pass. You should find your happiness inside yourself. Don't follow the worldly pleasure, my friend."

"Hold on for a jiffy," said Karan, looking more confused than ever. "For a while, I seemed to have understood you, but now you have lost me again. On one hand, you are saying that I should withdraw my senses like someone who wants nothing from the world. And on the other, you are saying that I should fight against my teachers for my pleasure?"

"The truth is," said Krish, "that there is no 'better path.' Both the path of action and the path of knowledge work just as well."

"I am still confused, brave one."

"Ho! ho! You will understand what I mean if you listen here. Your job is to do what you are meant to do, ok?"

"I got it, but I am still not convinced pal."

"Do you remember about the brave warriors of history? I have told one of them about this as well."

"What?" spoke a visibly shocked Karan. "I know we are no longer babies, but how on Earth could you have talked to our warriors, Krish? Tell me you are joking."

"I have lived many lives before this one, and you have as well. The difference is that you don't remember your past lives, but I do."

Karan stared at his friend as big tears rolled out of his rosy cheeks. They were tears of happiness. It was the divine Lord explaining to him. He went on his knees, joined his hands, and stayed there. Frozen! Completely frozen!

THE CONVERSATION IS STILL NOT OVER!

"Sacrifice your feelings to your sister, Karan, and the goodwill. Then find a way," Krish continued. "Those people you are worried for are already dead in their hearts. And I would also like to tell you that the soul never dies, it only changes its form. Let us take an example. So, your house is old now and you need a new one. Just like you changed your house, the soul changes the body."

"Krish, my friend." Karan was still frozen, the only thing moving was his mouth. "I am sorry, please forgive me! We were friends since I was two years old. I am sorry for the fights we had till now."

Karan started to feel guilty. If Krish was the real Lord, then Karan should have treated him with a lot more respect, but instead, he has been arguing and disagreeing with him. What was wrong with him?

A desire started overcoming Karan. "Please Krish, I know you are the divine God, but can you please show me your real form?"

"Of course. But I should give your eyes a speck of magical dust, so you can see the reality of me." A bright yellow light shook and Krish stood up, showing he was the real avatar of Lord Vishnu. That was a beautiful sight.

"Wow!" spoke Karan. "I understand that you are the divine God, and I also understand that I should use my mind to think a way of getting those bad teachers out of the way."

Karan and Krish stood up. "Time to get investigating," motivated Krish.

Karan already had a fantastic idea. He whispered it to Krish, and Krish smiled.

Then Karan ran to his parents to tell them to come to his school, and called the headmaster. Meanwhile, Krish called all the children from the school.

Can you guess what the plan is readers?

The Plan Works

After they had called everyone, Karan went to Mrs. Sarah and Mr. Tumpkin and said, "I quit. You guys are the best and are the winners. I can't beat you. You can give me any punishment you want."

"Ha!" spoke Mr. Tumpkin. "Now you will be kidnapped, just like your sister. Are you ready to go where she went?"

"Your choice. I have given up."

"I know what you have done. You silly children can't control us." Suddenly, they heard loud claps and the headmaster came in front. "Well done Karan, you have saved our school. Thank you so much."

"You got tricked, Mr. Tumpkin," giggled Krish.

"No! No! That cannot happen, sorry!" begged Mrs. Sarah.

Karan took the lead. "Do you know why I got the detention Mr. Raffle? It is because of the rules. They were changed by Mr. Tumpkin."

"Mr. Tumpkin, get your round pumpkin belly in the prison now," teased Mr. Raffle.

NEE! NAH!

The police came and got Mr. Tumpkin and Mrs. Sarah in the prison. But Karan was still impatient. He was looking for his sister. Then suddenly he caught sight of her. "Sis, here you are, I missed you so much."

"You have got me now, champ." smiled Tanya.

Karan ran home and hugged his best mate—and the divine soul.

Happiness Returns

"Welcome back, Tanya," announced Mr. Khanna, Tanya's father. Karan got overexcited and gave Tanya a necklace, not made from pearls but something more precious… a necklace of his hands. He hugged her for five whole minutes.

Sadness disappeared from everybody's faces and people were dancing and singing.

But Krish came to Karan and told him to come with him, and then said, "Let us ring the bells of other people's houses. I am getting bored."

Karan stood there feeling shocked. Krish was the divine God, but he still wanted to play!

"Come on then," cheered Karan…

THE END

Made in the USA
Monee, IL
03 May 2026

49438540R00030